The Little Red Hen

Story by Nikki Gamble

Illustrated by Scott Nash

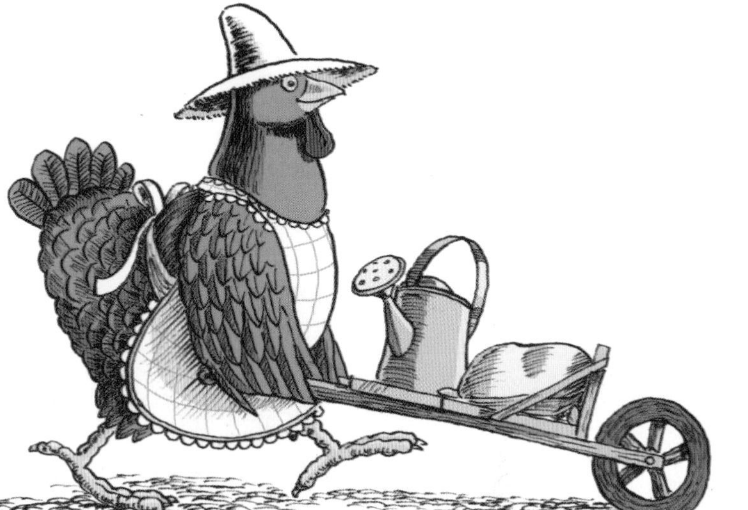

OXFORD

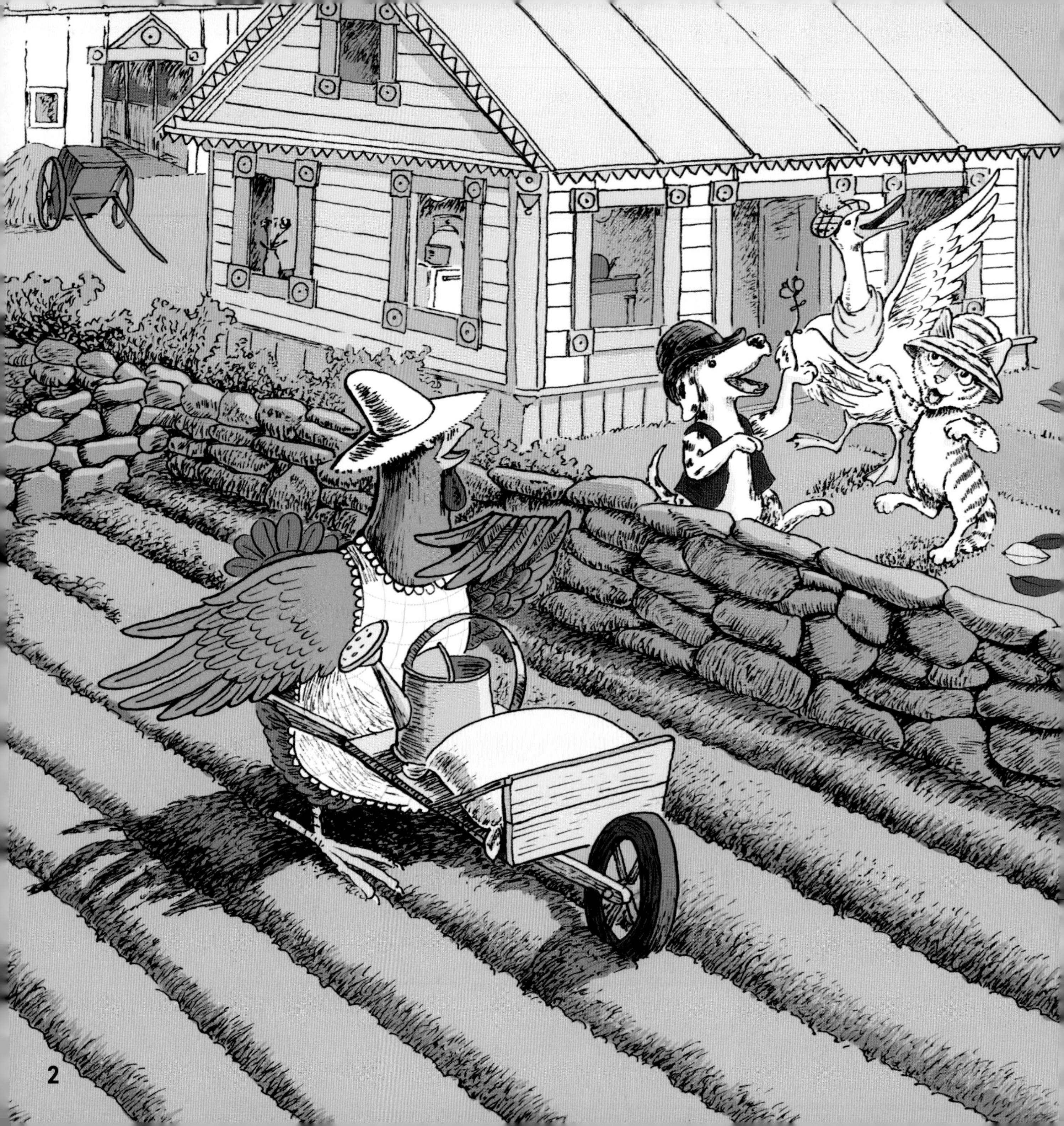

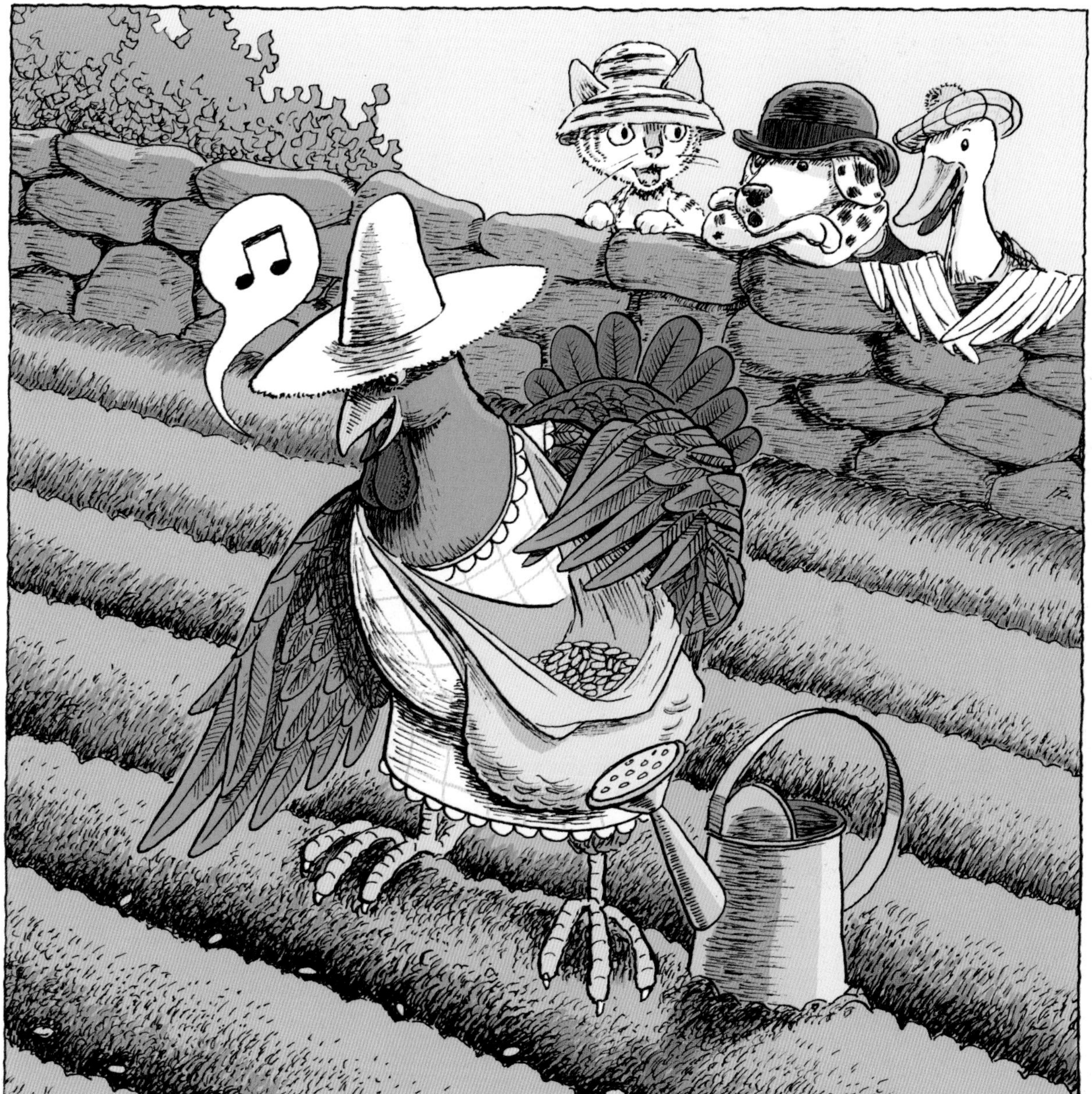

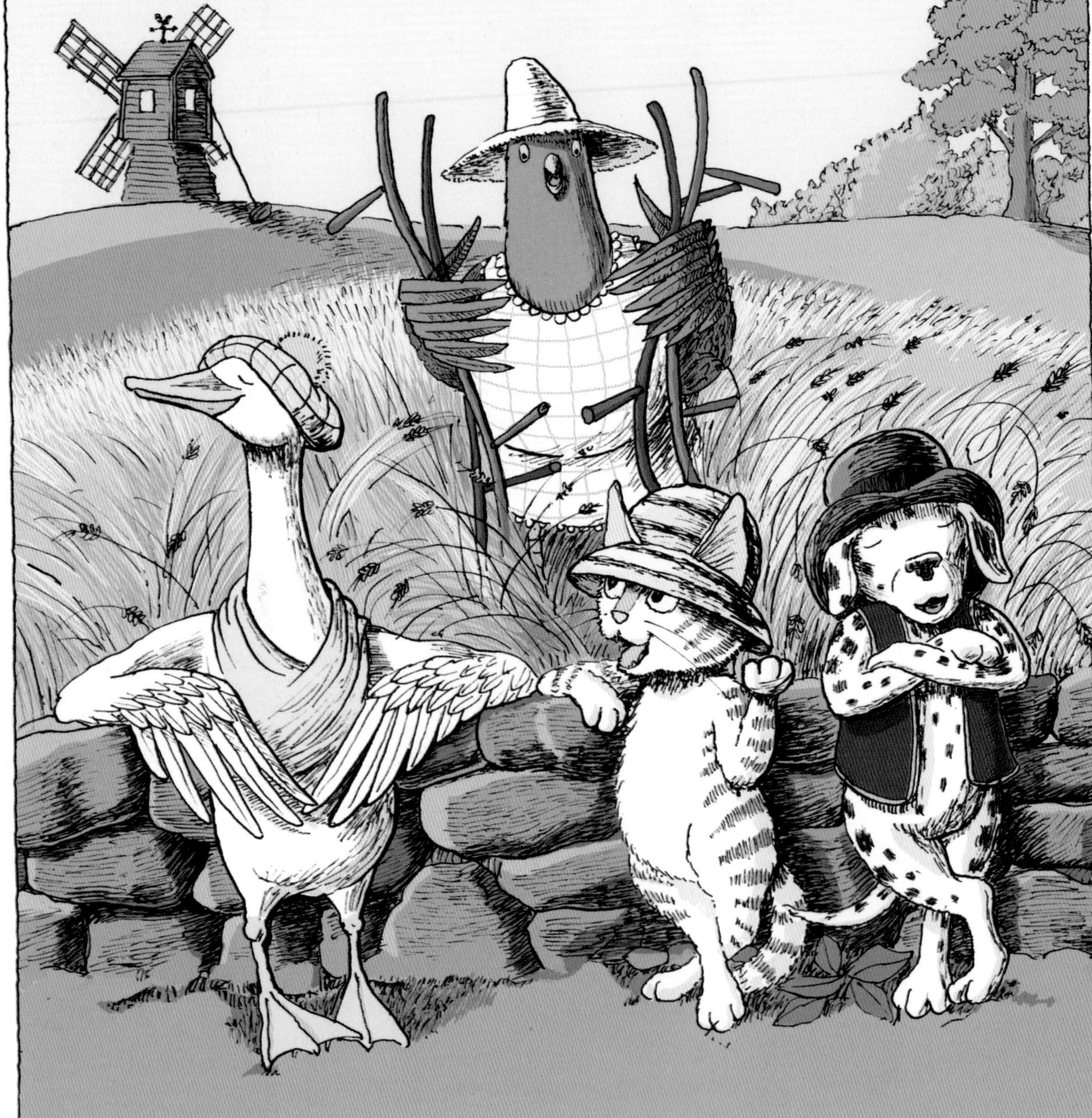

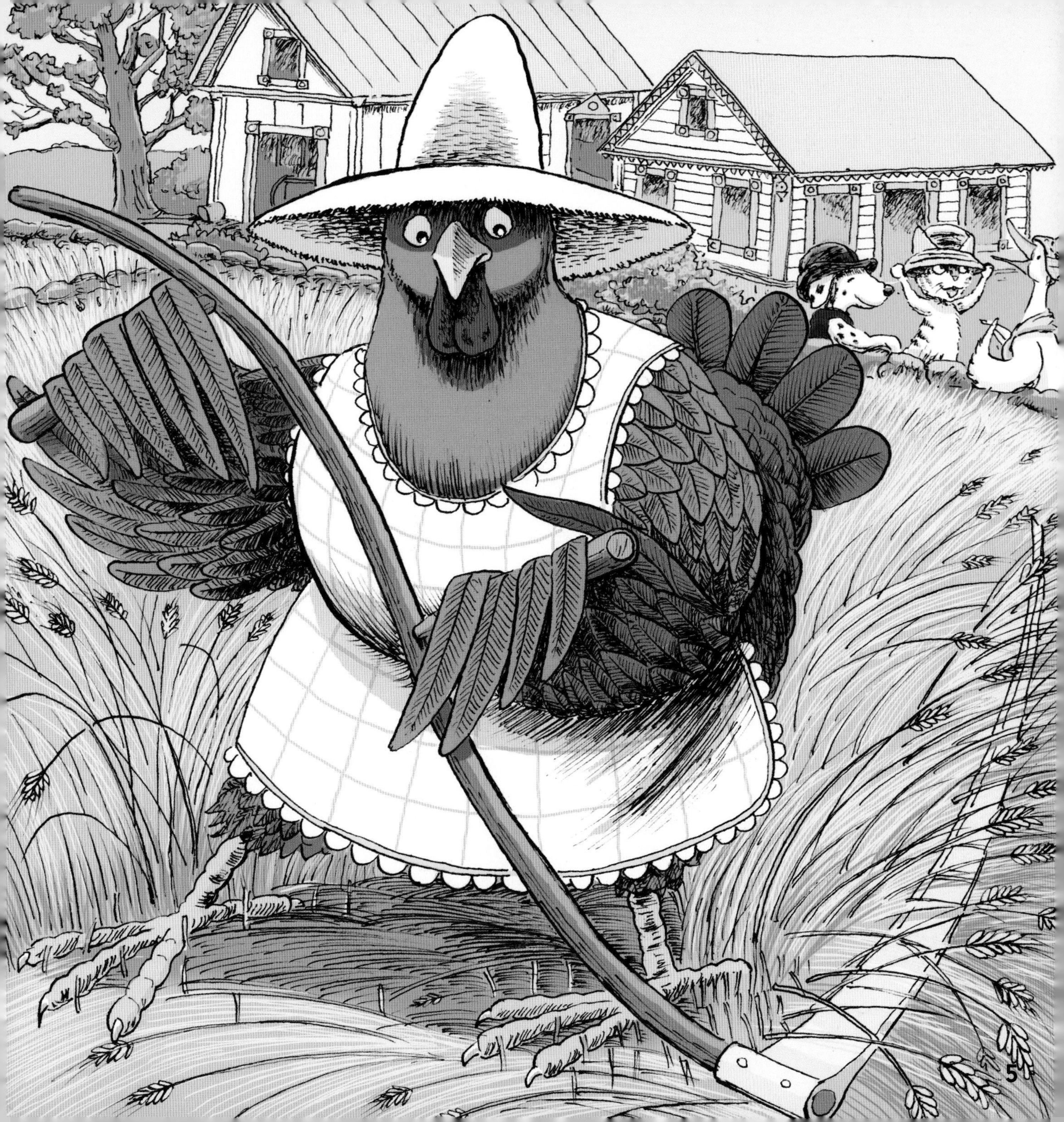

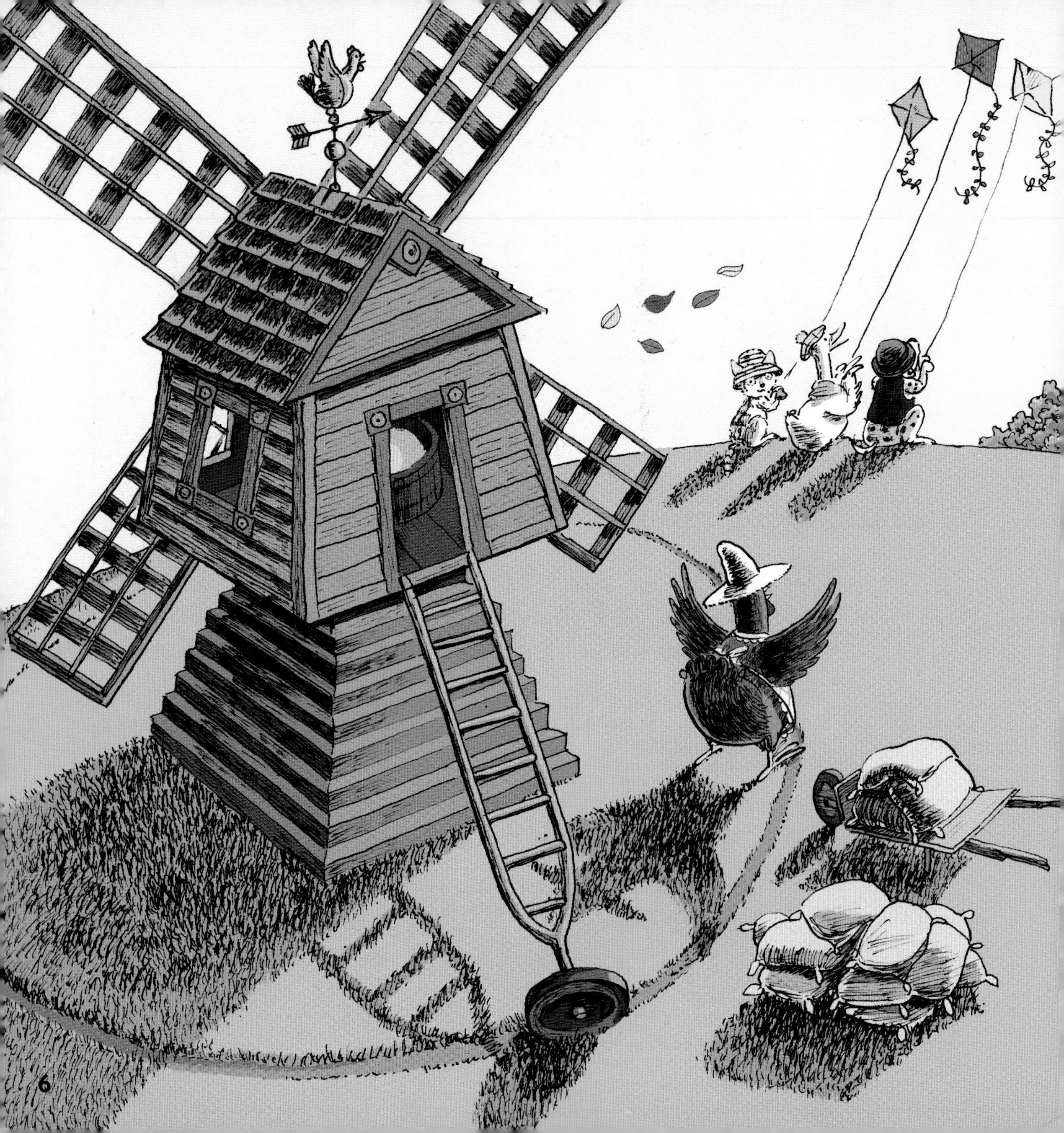

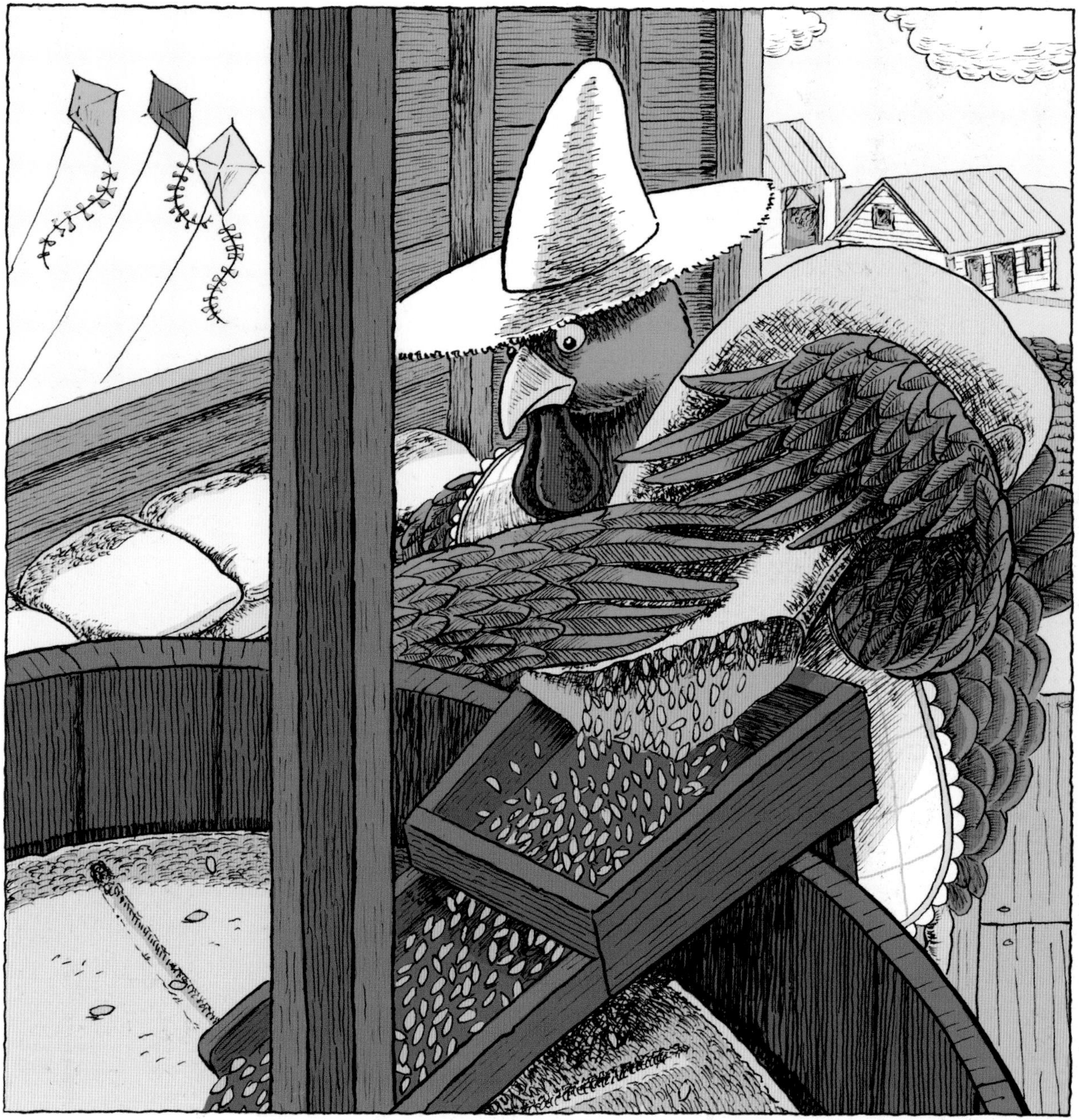

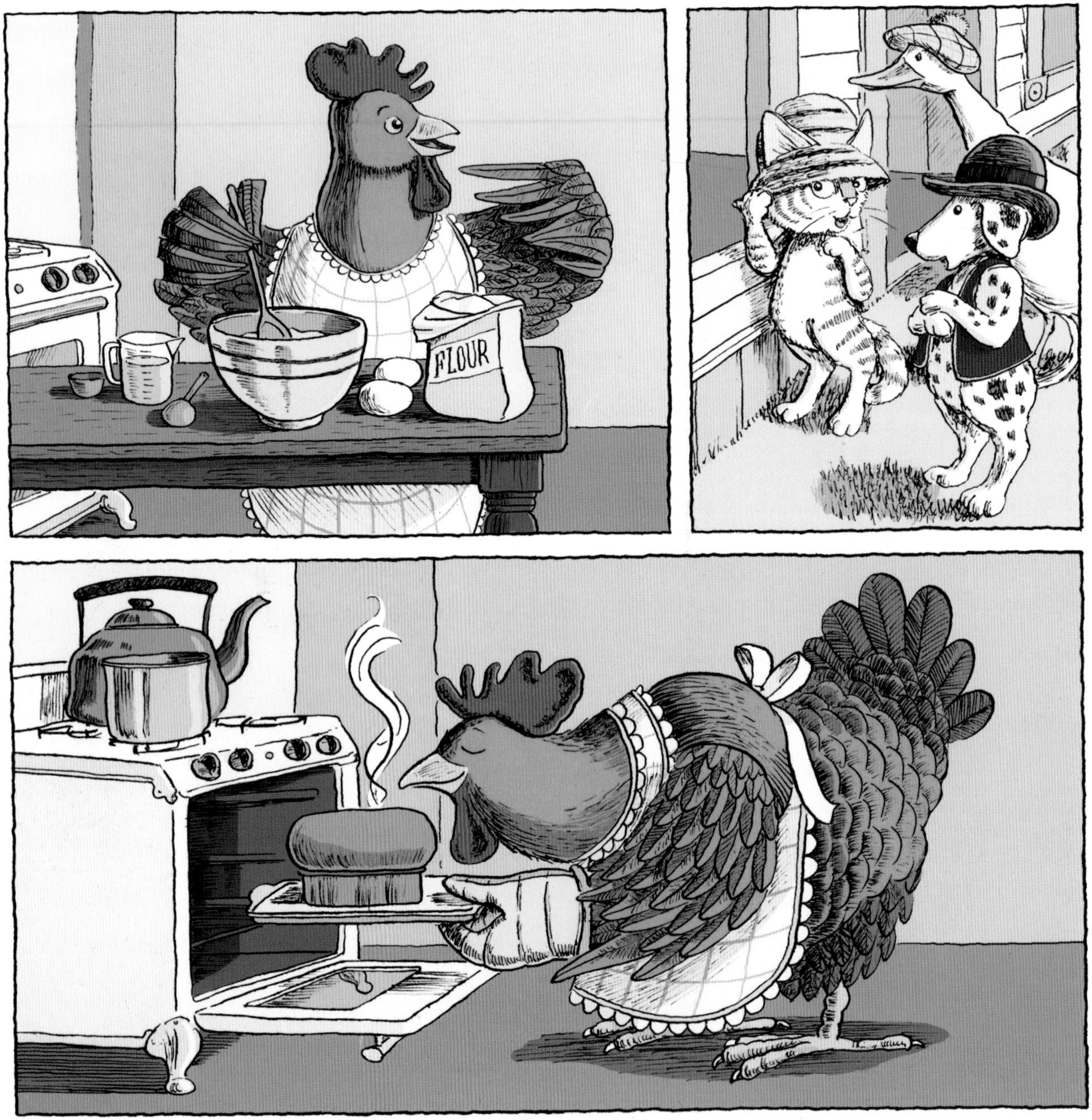
FLOUR

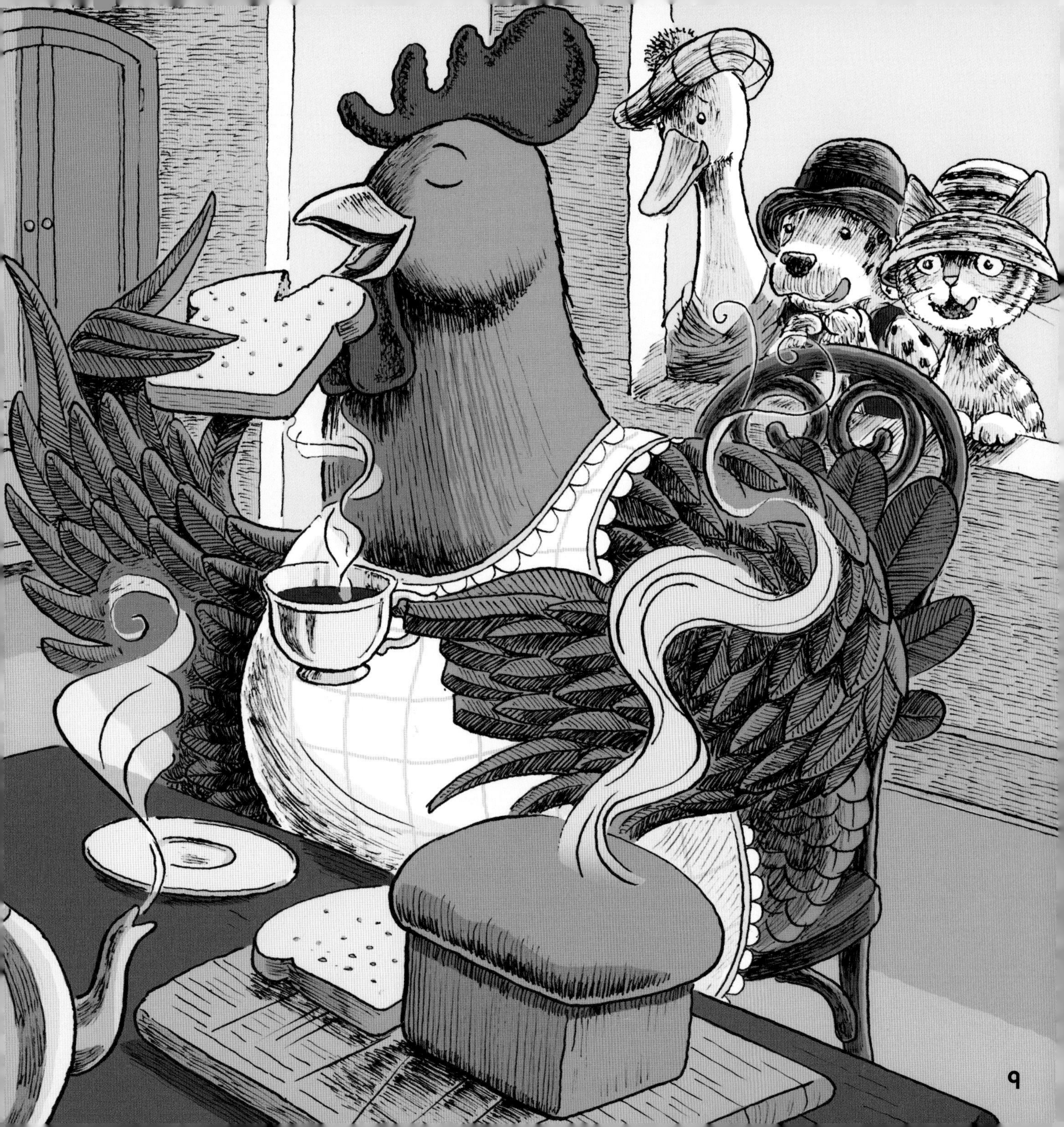

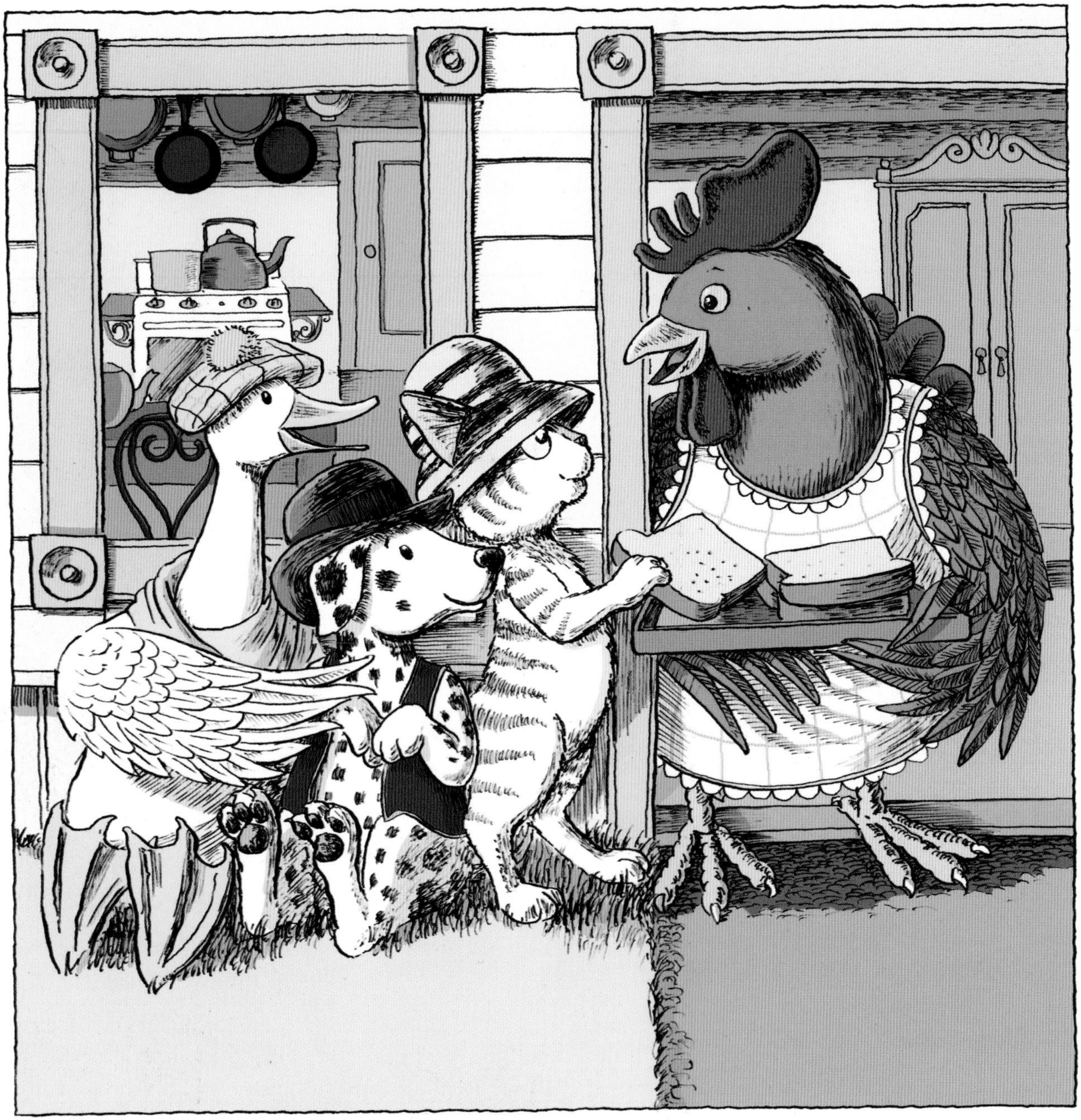

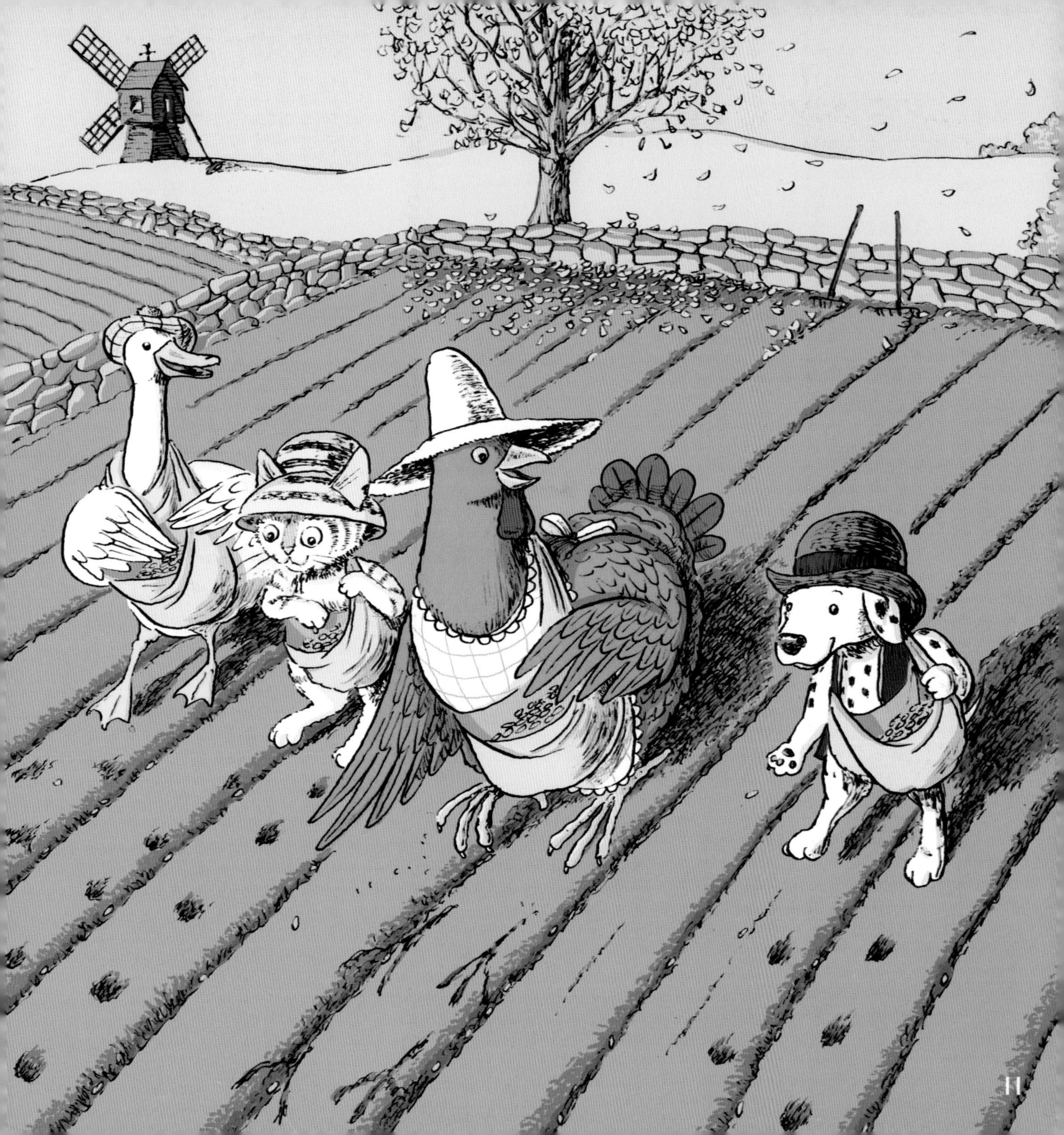

Retell the story

Once upon a time...

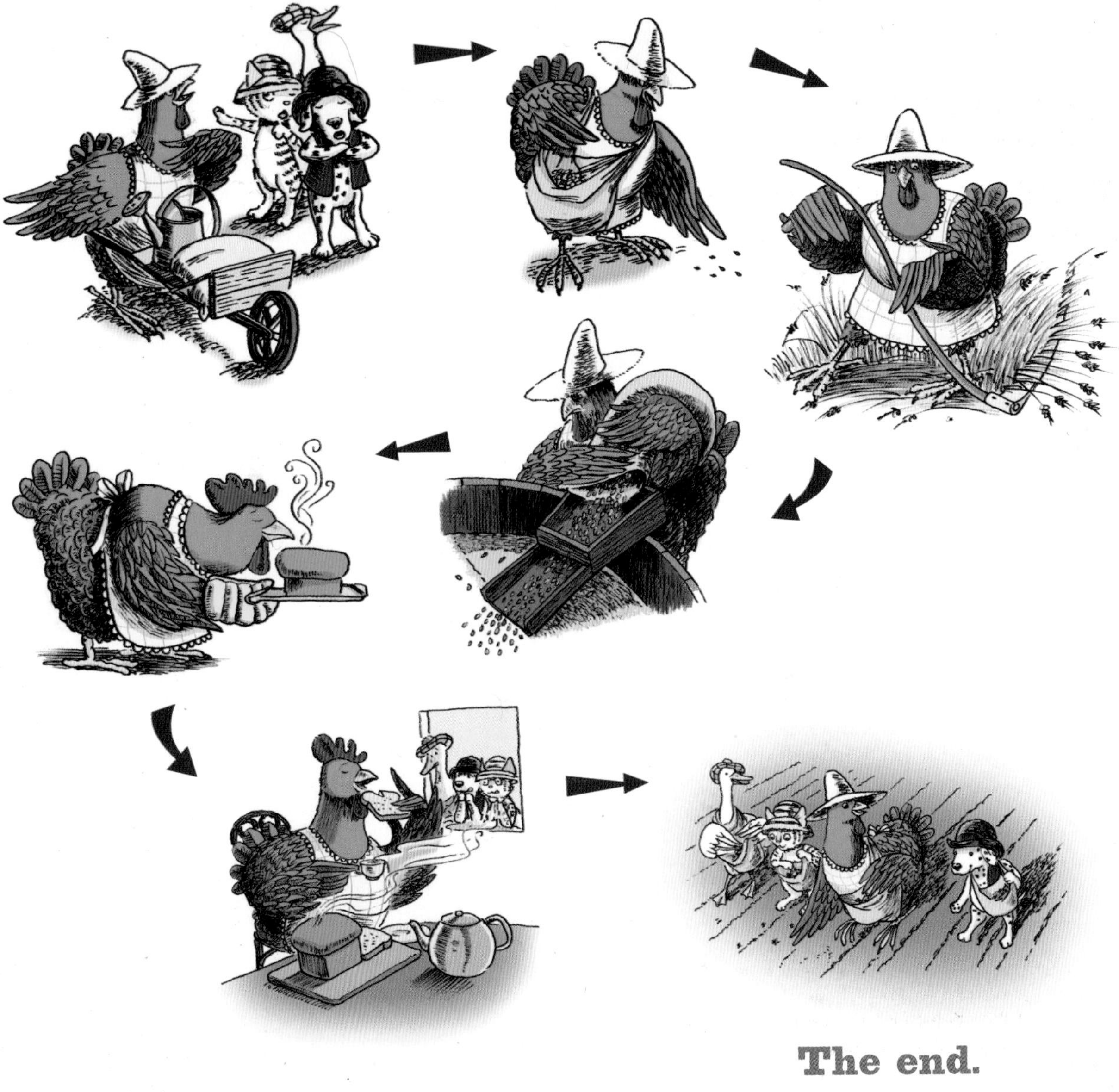

The end.